The
WILL JAMES
Cowboy Book

A LETTER FROM WILL JAMES

Dear Boys and Girls:

It seems as if lots of people want to know about cowboys and their work. I get letters with questions about the range country, the cowboy, riding, handling cattle. So I made this book which answers questions about cowboys and tells stories about them.

If you know something about cowboys and horses, roping and branding, why, start with the stories. But, if you don't, I'd say for you to start with the section called "On the Ranch with Uncle Bill." Then read the stories. You will know something about us, our work, our horses and our country before you get through.

I've done it all very sincerely and for you.

The
WILL JAMES
Cowboy Book

Will James

MOUNTAIN PRESS PUBLISHING COMPANY
Missoula, Montana
2003

Cover Art and Frontispiece: *I Wanted to See a Cowboy Stretch His Rope on a Range Critter* (alternate title: *Roping a Range Critter*). Oil on canvas, 1932. From the permanent collection of the Yellowstone Art Museum, Billings, Montana. Reprinted with permission of the Will James Art Company.

Tumbleweed is a registered trademark of
Mountain Press Publishing Company

Originally edited by Alice Dalgliesh of Scribners in 1938

Library of Congress Cataloging-in-Publication Data
James, Will, 1892-1942.
    The Will James cowboy book / Will James.
       p. cm. — (Tumbleweed series)
    Originally published: New York : Scribner, c1938.
    Summary: A collection of stories and art from Will James, who grew up on a ranch and wrote many books about his experiences at the end of the nineteenth and beginning of the twentieth century.
    ISBN 0-87842-469-5 (casebound : alk. paper)
    1. James, Will, 1892-1942—Anecdotes—Juvenile literature. 2. Cowboys—West (U.S.)—Biography—Anecdotes—Juvenile literature. 3. Ranch life—West (U.S.)—Anecdotes—Juvenile literature. 4. West (U.S.)—Social life and customs—Anecdotes—Juvenile literature. 5. Cowboys—West (U.S.)—Pictorial works—Juvenile literature. 6. Ranch life—West (U.S.)—Pictorial works—Juvenile literature. 7. West (U.S.)—Social life and customs—Pictorial works—Juvenile literature. [1. James, Will, 1892-1942. 2. Cowboys. 3. Ranch life—West (U.S.) 4. West (U.S.)—Social life and customs.] I. Title. II. Series: James, Will, 1892-1942. Tumbleweed series.
F596.J265 2003
813'.52—dc21
                                       2002013967

Printed in Canada

MOUNTAIN PRESS PUBLISHING COMPANY
P.O. Box 2399
Missoula, Montana 59806
(406) 728-1900

BOOKS BY WILL JAMES

Cowboys North and South, *1924*

The Drifting Cowboy, *1925*

Smoky, the Cowhorse, *1926*

Cow Country, *1927*

Sand, *1929*

Lone Cowboy, *1930*

Sun Up, *1931*

Big-Enough, *1931*

Uncle Bill, *1932*

All in the Day's Riding, *1933*

The Three Mustangeers, *1933*

Home Ranch, *1935*

Young Cowboy, *1935*

In the Saddle with Uncle Bill, *1935*

Scorpion, *1936*

Cowboy in the Making, *1937*

Flint Spears, *1938*

Look-See with Uncle Bill, *1938*

The Will James Cowboy Book, *1938*

The Dark Horse, *1939*

Horses I Have Known, *1940*

My First Horse, *1940*

The American Cowboy, *1942*

Will James Book of Cowboy Stories, *1951*

Publisher's Note

Will James's books represent an American treasure. His writing and drawings introduced generations of captivated readers to the lifestyle and spirit of the American cowboy and the West. Following James's death in 1942, the reputation of this remarkable artist and writer languished, and nearly all of his twenty-four books went out of print. But in recent years, interest in James's work has surged, due in part to the publication of several biographies and film documentaries, public exhibitions of James's art, and the formation of the Will James Society.

Now, in conjunction with the Will James Art Company of Billings, Montana, Mountain Press Publishing Company is reprinting each of Will James's classic books in handsome cloth and paperback editions. The new editions contain all the original artwork and text, feature an attractive new design, and are printed on acid-free paper to ensure many years of reading pleasure. They are published under the name the Tumbleweed Series.

The republication of Will James's books would not have been possible without the help and support of the many fans of Will James. Because all James's books and artwork remain under copyright protection, the Will James Art Company has been instrumental in providing the necessary permissions and furnishing artwork. Special care has been taken to keep each volume in the Tumbleweed Series faithful to the original vision of Will James.

The Will James Society was formed in 1992 as a nonprofit organization dedicated to preserving the memory and works of Will James. The society is one of the primary catalysts behind a growing interest in not only Will James and his work, but also the life and heritage of the working cowboy. For more information on the society, contact:

WILL JAMES SOCIETY
c/o Will James Art Company
2237 Rosewyn Lane • Billings, Montana 59102

Mountain Press is pleased to make Will James's books available again. Read and enjoy!

Contents

A Young Cowboy

THESE STORIES about Billy are all stories about me. I was that boy Billy and a cowboy from the very start. My dad was a cowboy before me.

Some of the stories say "I" and some say "Bill" or "Billy," but it's all the same boy.

WILL JAMES '30

They rode all day.

BILLY GOES TO THE ROUND-UP

ONE DAY DURING THE FALL Billy's dad told him to saddle up, that he was going to take him along to where the round-up wagon was camped, fifteen miles or so away.

Billy didn't stop to ask questions or to have the words said over. He grabbed his clothes, lit out the door as if the house was afire, and went full-speed ahead for the corrals. He had caught his horse Big Enough and was slipping the saddle on him by the time his dad opened the corral gate.

Ten circuses couldn't have made any kid happier than Billy was at the thought of seeing the round-up outfit. He'd heard his dad tell of such outfits many a time and of the work that went on.

They rode all day and Billy got to see further than he'd ever had a chance to see from the home ranch. Presently they came to the round-up camp on the creek against the willows.

Billy and his dad picketed their horses to graze close by and went into the camp. Billy followed his father through the rolls of bedding up to where the cowmen were gathered, busy talking things over.

Being among all those men made Billy a little shy at first. Some saw that he didn't like to be asked such questions as "How old are you, Sonny?" or "Can you read a brand yet?" So they began asking him more grown-up questions like,

"How did the stock winter in your country?" or "What make of saddle are you riding, Boy?" It made him feel right proud to answer these questions, especially when they asked him about his saddle.

Finally the men left Billy to himself, and after he had listened to their talk for a spell he started to roam around the camp. He watched the cowboys come in, unsaddle, rope their night horses and picket them here and there on good grass. Billy watched the whole performance, and with watching other things around, it looked sometimes as if he'd about twist his head off.

There were around thirty riders in camp when the cook hollered "Come and get it, you hyenas, or I'll throw it out." Tin plates, cups, knives and forks, salt and pepper and sugar were on the drop board of the chuck box; good hunks of range beef were in Dutch ovens; and in the other ovens were browned potatoes, hot biscuits, and gravy in the skillet.

There was no rush. Every rider waited for the other to take the lead, help himself, and take his time about it. All were hungry, but there was no pushing and shoving.

Billy had sidled up to his dad and watched how one rider after another helped himself to plate and cup and grub. When his time came he did it like a man, so much like a man that nobody thought of helping him. His plate and cup filled, he picked a place where he could be by himself and watch the whole bunch. There on the sod he squatted like any good cowboy and began to get away with all he'd piled on the plate that rested between his knees.

Along about sundown one of the cowboys dug out his mouth organ and began playing songs that were sung all

4

The chuck wagon

about the cow country at the time when the buffalo roamed over it. Many old timers picked up the tunes and went to humming, and then one cowboy and another started singing, or tried to.

At last the fire burned low, the mouth organ was put away, the singing stopped, and riders began to scatter out to their beds, unroll them and crawl in. His father, seeing Billy so wide awake and interested in everything, thought he'd let the boy have a night of it. Instead of telling him to

5

come to bed he just pointed out where the bed would be, telling him to come when he was ready. It was almost midnight before Billy came to where his dad was, and crawled in.

It seemed to Billy that he'd no more than just turned in when the cook's loud holler was heard. He didn't budge for a while. Pretty soon he heard the crackling of the fire and then voices coming from here and there. The camp soon came to life.

It didn't take long for Billy to dress. All he'd taken off when he crawled into bed was his hat and coat and his overalls and boots. He was up, washed and alongside his dad before the cook told the crowd to "go to it, cowboys," and it didn't take him long to get his breakfast down.

Every rider in camp was at the herd when Billy and Big-Enough got there. It was the biggest herd that'd been put in one bunch that year, and numbered around four thousand head. It was pretty nearly too big a herd to work all at once, but with all the riders on hand it could be done. So the work started. The cattle belonging to the big outfit were cut out first because they made up more than half the herd. Then each neighboring cowman and his riders took their turn cutting out their own cattle from the strays there were left. When one cowman was through, he took his cattle far enough to one side so there wouldn't be a chance of any getting away and mixing with the herd. Then, leaving one rider with them, he'd ride back to the main herd and help the others.

Billy had quite a time keeping out of the way when he first rode up to the herd. If a critter came towards him he'd try to dodge and give it a clear run. Then he'd turn his horse the wrong way and the animal would go back in the herd.

Billy liked to see the ropers do their work.

So his dad rode up to him and told him to keep his horse still and the critter wouldn't notice him.

"There's only one thing," said his dad. "Keep away from fighting bulls, because the one that gets whipped don't care much what he goes through when he makes his get-away, and your horse might be in his way."

There were lots of bulls fighting in that big herd. Billy watched the way each man and horse worked. Once in a while there'd be some argument among the cowmen as to a brand on a certain critter. The brand would be dim, or crooked, or blotched so it couldn't be read very well. One would say it was this and the other would say it was that. There was only one way to try and settle such arguments, and that was to rope and throw the animal. Then the hair was ruffled and the brand and earmark was looked at close.

Billy liked to see the ropers do their work on the big cattle, for the big cattle sure could hit the end of a rope and make it sing like a fiddle-string, and a couple of times a horse was jerked down.

It was along about the middle of the forenoon, or a little after, when the whole herd was worked and the strays were claimed by their owners. An early meal was spread. All hands took to it, and then, after a lot of handshaking and "I'll see you next year" or "At shipping time," the cowmen and their riders started for home.

8

BILLY BREAKS HIS FIRST BRONC

B ILLY WAS A BORN COWBOY; the only kind that ever
makes the real cowboy. One day his dad told him he
could have a certain black horse if he could break him. It
was a little black horse, pretty as a picture. Billy went wild
at the sight of him, and ran into the corral to get as close
a view of the horse as he could.

"By golly!" he said. "I've always wanted to break in a
horse. That'll be lots of fun."

The next morning Billy's father found Billy in the corral
with the new horse.

"Well, I see you're busy right early, Billy."

"You bet," he said. "He's some horse!"

"He sure is," agreed his dad. "And your first bronc, too."

An hour or so later, after a lot of handling, Billy had his
saddle on the black horse, and cinched to stay. By this time
quite a few of the cowboys had gathered around. The fore-
man, the cowboys, all the ranch hands were watching. All
was set but taking the hobbles off the horse's front feet and
climbing on. Some of the men offered to do that for Billy
but that young cowboy said no. He wanted to do it all himself;
it was his bronc.

Billy gathered his hackamore rope reins and a hunk of
mane to go with it. Then he grabbed the saddle horn with

his right hand and, sticking his foot in the stirrup, eased himself into the saddle. He squirmed around until he was well set, saw that the length of the reins between his hands and the pony's head was just right, then he reached over and pulled off the blindfold.

Billy's lips were closed tight; he was ready for whatever happened. The pony blinked at seeing daylight again, looked back at the boy sitting on him, snorted, and trotted off.

A laugh went up from all around. Billy turned a blank face toward his father and hollered,

"Hey, Dad, he won't buck!"

Another laugh was heard and when it quieted down, his father spoke up.

"Never mind, Son," he said, trying to keep a straight face, "he might buck yet."

The words were no more than out of his mouth, when the little black lit into bucking. Billy was loosened the first jump for he'd been paying more attention to what his dad was saying than to what he was sitting on. The little pony crowhopped around the corral and bucked just enough to keep the kid from getting back in the saddle. Billy was hanging on to all he could find, but pretty soon the little old pony happened to make the right kind of a jump for the kid and he straightened up again.

Billy rode pretty fair the next few jumps and managed to keep his seat pretty well under him, but he wasn't satisfied with just sitting there; he grabbed his hat and began fanning. All went fine for a few more jumps and then trouble broke loose. For the little horse of a sudden really went to bucking. Billy dropped his hat and made a wild grab for the saddle horn.

"Y-e-e-ep! I'm a wolf!"

But the hold on the saddle horn didn't help him any; he kept going, up and up he went, a little higher every jump, and pretty soon he started coming down. When he did come down he was by his lonesome. The horse had gone another way.

"Where is he?" said Billy, trying to get some of the earth out of his eyes.

"Right here, Son," said his father, who'd caught the horse and brought him up.

He handed the kid the hackamore reins and touched him on the hand.

"And listen here, young fellow, if I catch you grabbing the horn with that paw of yours again, I'll tie it and the other right back where you can't use 'em."

Those few words hit the kid pretty hard. There was a frown on his face and his lips were quivering at the same time. He was both ashamed and peeved.

His father held the horse while Billy climbed on again.

"Are you ready, cowboy?"

After some efforts the kid smiled and answered, "Yes, Dad, let him go."

The pony lit into bucking the minute he was loose this time and seemed to mean business from the start. Time and again Billy's hand reached down as if to grab the saddle horn, but he kept away from it.

The little horse was bucking pretty hard, and for a kid Billy was doing mighty fine, but the horse still proved too much for him. Billy kept getting further and further away from the saddle till finally he slid along the pony's shoulder and to the ground once again.

The kid was up before his dad could get to him and he began looking for his horse right away.

"I don't think you'd better try to ride him any more today, Sonny," his father said, as he brushed some of the dust off the kid's clothes. "Maybe tomorrow you can ride him easy."

But Billy turned and saw the horse daring him, it seemed. So he crossed the corral, caught the black, blindfolded him and climbed him again.

Then his dad walked up to Billy and said so nobody else could hear, "You go after him this time, Billy, and just make this pony think you're the wolf of the world. Paw him the same as you did that last calf you rode."

"Y-e-e-ep!" Billy hollered as he jerked the blind off the pony's eyes. "I'm a wolf!"

Billy was a wolf, he was pawing the black from ears to rump. Daylight showed plenty between him and the saddle but somehow he managed to stick on and stay right side up. The horse, surprised at the change, finally let up on his bucking; he was getting scared and had found a sudden hankering to start running.

After that it was easy for Billy; he rode him around the corral a couple of times and then, all smiles and proud as a peacock, he climbed off.

Billy had ridden his first bronc.

A BEAR ON THE ROOF

THE WINTER BOPY, the old French Canadian trapper, and I spent in his main camp was the time he taught me to use a rifle.

The rifle was one of those muzzle loaders and about two feet taller than I was. Bopy was very careful in showing me how to load it. He gave me advice about the right way to handle a gun and about the dangerous end of it. Then he told me to go out and bring home the bacon.

Most every day, while Bopy was gone to set his traps, I'd strap my snowshoes on my moccasins, take my long rifle and go hunting. It wasn't that I liked to hunt, but I wanted some change from moose meat. Big white snowshoe rabbits were about all I saw, and once in a while I'd get one. I didn't get a chance at anything bigger because the bears had all gone to sleep for the winter. And Bopy had warned me not to shoot at big animals.

But I did get mixed up with a bear once. It was after a long warm spell. The warm weather made one bear wake up early and he went out hunting.

There was a snowbank alongside the lean-to where we kept the meat and the bear climbed up on that snowbank on top of the lean-to. I heard him sniff and paw up there. He was sure heavy because even through that thick roof I

I would go hunting.

could tell just where he planted a paw. Then he must have got a whiff of the meat that was in the lean-to, because he kept hanging around there, climbing up and down and clawing. He'd circle around and sniff and I got to thinking of the window. There was no glass in the window, only oiled paper. I hadn't closed the shutter and all he'd have to do would be to stick his nose to the paper and it'd fall apart. I knew he'd come in then, so as to get to that meat, and I waited for him.

15

I reached for my rifle, not knowing that the birdshot it was loaded with would only annoy him if I did hit him at long distance. Anyway, I waited a spell, hoping he would stick his nose through that window. But he didn't. Instead he quit his circling and began tearing at the lean-to roof as if he sure enough meant to get that meat. He made plenty of noise and I got to thinking he wasn't doing the dugout any good, so I got up and slipped on my moccasins. I was all dressed but those, and I opened the door and went out. But I couldn't see the bear and all I could get of his where-abouts was sniffs and grunts. The snow was pretty deep and I couldn't get around very fast, but when I got around the lean-to I met him. He looked like a mountain.

I don't think the barrel of my rifle was over a foot from his nose when I pulled the trigger. Bopy had often told me always to stick the barrel away ahead and be ready for work when I really wanted to use it. It was ahead that night and I pulled the trigger at just a good time.

When Bopy came back two days later and I told him about the bear he grinned at me sort of proud-like and said words that made me feel good. He said I'd held down the camp and saved the grub and that bears "was awful pests." But if Bopy was surprised and pleased at me getting up in the middle of the night and chasing the bear away, he was more than surprised when he began to track him the next day. He hadn't gone over half a mile from the camp when he found him stretched out and frozen stiff. That little bird shot at close range had nearly punctured his head through.

Bopy had never thought that I'd killed the bear and neither did I, but there he was. When I came up to answer

Bopy's holler and saw that big hairy creature stretched out on the snow, I didn't know what to think or say. Bopy said something about a mighty lucky shot and advised me never to try that again with one of those big fellows.

That bear hide would have covered the whole floor of our dugout. It sure was a nice color, too.

He found the bear stretched out and frozen stiff.

THE PET WOLVES

THE CAMP WE STRUCK the next winter was quite a camp. It had two rooms and was furnished with things not made out of hewed timber. There were a lot of knickknacks around, too, and pictures of people and some books and things.

I found out that this was Bopy's *one* main camp. It was his home and only about a hundred miles south of where he was born. That camp with all that was in it had a whole lot to do with keeping me contented that winter. There were plenty of books and some blank paper. I could read and draw all I pleased. Then, to make things nicer, I had a couple of pets to keep me company while Bopy was out on his trap line.

My two pets were wolves. The man who brought up our stuff had got them out of a den that spring and tried to work them in with his dog team. They didn't turn out as well as sled dogs and he was going to kill them soon as their fur was good. Bopy bargained for them and here I was with two big gray fellows following me around. They were well trained and minded me. I didn't take to my pets very much at first, but they sure took to me and wouldn't have much to do with Bopy. If they did anything I didn't like I'd kick 'em in the ribs, and all they'd do was whine and lie down and beg for me to quit. It strikes me funny when I think of that, because either one of those wolves would just have had to snap at me once and I'd not have been able to touch them again. Gray wolves have powerful jaws, and when they stood up on each side of me their withers weren't so far below my shoulders.

One time Bopy got peeved at something the wolves had done. He hunted them up and began to work on them. I came about just about when Bopy would soon have been getting the worst of it. He'd got himself a limb off a tree, but it was breaking. Little me ran in and busted up the fight. I kicked each wolf in the jaw and they hunted for a hole as if a ghost was after them. Bopy looked at me sort of funny and then he grinned. I had all the handling of the wolves after that.

But kicks weren't all the wolves got from me. The three of us had a lot of fun together. We'd go a-hunting, me with my long rifle and the wolves with their speed and killing power. Sometimes they'd leave me and be gone for hours. They'd be chasing something and come back all gauntled up. In that time I'd killed some meat for them and lots of times they'd catch up with me while I was skinning whatever I killed. They'd crowd around me, their long red tongues hanging, but they never tried to reach for what I had, because they knew what they'd get would be a smack on their long nose. So they'd wait until I got ready and sort of back up against me while waiting. That was their way of hurrying me. A wolf never shows affection—he never licks at a person's face and hands as a dog would and he never wags his tail. The most he does to be friendly is lay his ears back and show a grin and try to look pleasant in that way, like a wolf.

The wolves were a lot of company to me.

The wolves were a lot of company to me that winter. I called them Gros and Otay. They'd lie by me while I drew and read, and I'd never make a move but what they did, too. If I jumped up they'd jump up too, and bustle up and look at the door of the cabin and growl. They'd sure look mean at times and it wouldn't have been so good for anybody to open that door unless he was ready to shoot right quick. Bopy knew that, and he never came in from his trap lines like he used to. He'd whistle a bit first and after he thought I'd got through talking to the wolves he'd ease in, and the tone of his voice as he spoke to me had all to do with his welcome. They never got used to him because he'd be gone too long at a time.

Of course Bopy could have made away with the wolves mighty quick, but seeing how they were so much company for me he figured they were worth having around. Bopy would laugh when he'd see me and the two wolves all stretched out in front of the fireplace. I'd be drawing while one wolf's head was resting on my leg and the other on my neck.

I didn't care so much for the wolves. Maybe that was why they liked me. I'd kick them off and they'd come right back. I'd be drawing horses about then, as usual, and wolf skin wasn't what horse hide meant to me.

Sometimes I'd play the wolves were horses. I'd ride them, put hackamores on them, and even tried to make pack horses out of them. I'd tail one to the other, but they never worked well. They'd slip their packs or else pull out of the hackamore. I'd braided a four strand rope out of moose hide and I'd throw a loop at them once in a while. They soon got wise to that loop and made themselves hard to catch when they'd see me spread out one.

With that kind of play to hold me I don't think I missed my horses as much that winter as I did the winter before. But I often thought of my little black and sorrel when I threw my moose-hide rope, and I'd have to draw them once in a while to keep from being too lonely for them.

The winter wore on and about February time came along. Moose and caribou were drifting North and one night a pack of wolves went by on their trail. My two wolves were full size by then. They stood up when they heard the drawn out howl of one of their kind, and began to talk back in the same language. They were restless, and figuring on a way out, but I held them down that night. A few nights later, I was sound asleep when I heard something tear. It was the paper on the window, the paper we used instead of glass. My two wolves had jumped up on my bed and gone out.

I listened, and few seconds later I heard the long holler of a wolf pack. I knew then what had happened. I jumped up, slipped on my long coat and moccasins and went out the way my wolves went. I had my rifle with me and I was going to get my wolves back.

God helps the children and the ignorant, because if the pack had turned I couldn't have written this. I followed the snarling pack of wolves until I couldn't hear them any more. Then, by the night sun, I tracked them. I snowshoed and cried and snowshoed and cried some more. I cried because I was peeved to think that Gros and Otay could have left me. I was so peeved at the thought that I'd have been likely to take a shot at them. But, lucky for me, the pack didn't turn—I didn't see my wolves. They had gone with the wild bunch.

It was well along towards sun-up when I dragged my long rifle back into camp. Tears were frozen all along my parka, plum down to my moccasins. Bopy, all eyes and worried, opened the door. He knew what had happened and he spoke softly as he pulled off my cap, unbuttoned my coat, and brought me near the fire.

"Tout est bien, mon enfant" ("all is well, my child"), he said. He slapped me on the shoulder and looked down at me and grinned. "Tu vas avoir tes chevaux bien vite maintenant" ("you're going to have your horses pretty soon, now").

Those words made me perk up, and it wasn't long before I began to ask Bopy questions as to how quick that would be. Bopy said, "Bien vite" (pretty soon), and I was put to bed. But I was still hurt. Gros and Otay shouldn't have left me the way they did. I went to sleep on that.

I woke up in a bad humor the next morning. I tracked my wolves some more, but it was no use. By the time I doubled back I think I'd have shot them on sight for running off the way they did . . . I never saw them any more.

A Cowboy's Year

MAYBE YOU'D LIKE TO KNOW what Bill did when he got to be a real cowboy. So I'll give you a bit about a cowboy's work and tell something of what he does every month in the year.

Some folks think it's easy being a cowboy, but that's not so. There's a lot of hard and dangerous work along with the fun.

JANUARY
Bucking the Snowdrifts

THE WINTER MONTHS in the cow country are hard. They take in a lot of bucking first one thing and then another. There are snowdrifts and blizzards.

In this case it's snow. The cowboy finds January one of the longest months of the year. When the snow is deep he has to keep riding and looking out for the weaker stock.

This picture tells how the rider is with his horse. The hand on the neck of the pony means "Steady, boy!" It shows that man and horse are *together* in the work.

Bucking the Snowdrifts

FEBRUARY
The End of a Killer

THE COWBOY has to be on the lookout for coyotes and wolves, so they won't kill the stock.

In this picture the cowboy is lucky. He has a few traps set where his day's riding takes him, and this time he's caught a big old gray boy, a wolf.

A cowboy doesn't kill an animal without a good reason. This wolf was a killer and did a lot of damage among the stock.

The End of a Killer

MARCH
The First Blades of Green

T HERE'S NO COUNTRY in the world where the first patch of green is thought as much of as it is in the range countries of the Northwest. Maybe I feel that way about it on account of the long winters I've put in there.

I well remember how it struck me when March would come along. On the sunny side of a ridge the snow melted away leaving a patch of warm earth and real green grass. I could seldom help letting out a glad war-whoop at the sight. And I'd slide my horse to a standstill right there.

That patch of green was there to say that old man Winter was giving away, and the whole world would soon be a-smiling again.

The First Blades of Green

APRIL
Gathering the Saddle Horses

THIS IS THE MONTH when the cowboys begin shedding off their heavy coats. They often wish before they get back to camp that they'd kept the coats on.

The riders are out gathering the saddle horses. The ponies have had many long months' rest and are not at all easy to catch up to and turn.

As the cowboy hazes the ponies towards the big corrals, he rides by many a cow that looks up at his coming but keeps a-chewing on tall blades of green. The little fellow that's at her side looks up, too, not knowing what all this horse-chasing is about. He doesn't know that these ponies will soon be packing riders to round up him and his kind.

Gathering the Saddle Horses

MAY
The Spring Round-Up

IF SPRING is not too slow in coming, the spring round-up starts in this month. A wagon goes out with grub and the cowboys' rolls of bedding. Wherever that wagon is, the riders gather when work is done. It is camp.

Following after the wagon comes what is called the "remuda," a herd of saddle horses for the riders.

In the spring round-up the new calves all get the markings and brand of the ranch the mother belongs to. In this picture that's just what is happening.

The Spring Round-Up

JUNE
The Horse Round-Up

EVERY GOOD SIZE COW-OUTFIT owns many horses, some of them up to thousands. It takes many horses to run a cow-outfit. Every rider is given from six to twelve of them at one time. Then at the ranches there's a lot of work. The ranch hands need many work-horses to put up the hay that's needed to carry the cattle through the winter.

The round-up of stock-horses (meaning brood mares and colts) starts after the cow work is over in the Spring. These horses are being rounded up so that the colts can be branded. Some of them may be kept at the home ranch for breaking.

The Horse Round-Up

JULY
Riding for a Prize

THERE'S NOT MUCH WORK on the range in July. It's kind of a good thing, too, on account of celebrations for the Fourth. Rodeos are held here and there and the range riders are the boys that make the rodeos what they are.

The cowboy in this picture is celebrating for all he's worth and at the same time riding for a prize. When the four-day celebration is over he'll go back to the range again.

Riding for a Prize

AUGUST
Breaking Broncs

HORSE-BREAKING comes pretty near being a year-round job, summer and winter.

The cowboy in this picture is "starting" his horse in the way most riders do. The pony's hind foot is tied so that he can't kick at the rider or act up too much when the saddle is slipped on his back. The rider puts the saddle on with one hand and with the other hand on the hackamore rope, he keeps the horse's head where it belongs. A simple twist of the wrist does the trick, if the twist is at the right time.

Breaking Broncs

SEPTEMBER
Line Riders

T HE LINE-RIDERS' JOB is to see that none of the company's cattle get out of their own land and no others stray in. The riders don't have to see the cattle every day to know where they are, tracks and other signs tell them. Line-riders also keep out the cattle thief. With a line rider on the job the thief's trail would be found within a few hours.

September brings line-riding pretty well to an end. Most of the riders leave their line camps at that time to join the round-up wagon. These two boys in the picture are trying to count the days until they can get back to the round-up wagon.

Line Riders

OCTOBER
Cutting Out

T HE FALL ROUND-UP is on full swing. Herds are gathered and late spring calves are branded. Then, with their mammies, they're driven to some corral where the calf is taken from his mother to be weaned. The "weaner" calf is five or six months old. He's had strong, rich milk all summer, and grass too, so he's more than husky now. He will be put on good grass so he'll stay that way.

With the fall branding and weaning there comes the beef-gathering. Fine big steers are brought to the cutting grounds, cut out and put into the main herd. "Cutting out" means separating a critter from the rest of the bunch.

Cutting Out

NOVEMBER
The End of the Season

▼

T HE FALL ROUND-UP is over. The beef herd has been
driven to the shipping pens at the railroad and loaded
in the stock cars. The old stock has been brought close to
the feeding grounds and the work of the season with the
round-up wagon comes to an end.

Some of the boys are catching their private ponies, which
have had a long summer's rest. With his saddle on one horse
and his bed on another, the rider never cares much where
his trail ends. It'll be in some new country with a winter's
job breaking horses. Or it may be in some deserted cabin
setting a line of traps for coyotes and bobcats.

The End of the Season

DECEMBER
The Winter Camp

SOME OF THE RIDERS stay with a cow-outfit the year round. These are sent in pairs to the cabins or winter camps scattered by the creeks. They keep an eye on the stock that needs feeding. One or two ranch hands are there to feed the stock the riders bring in and sometimes there's a cook to help along.

As the winter sets in the work piles up and everyone is kept mighty busy. And the work goes on just the same if the sun is shining or a blizzard is howling. Christmas is only another day at a cow camp, but there's fun sometimes along with the work. The cowboy in the picture is bringing in a Christmas tree.

The Winter Camp–Christmas

Uncle Bill

On the Ranch
with Uncle Bill

THIS PART OF THE BOOK is to help you if you don't know all about the cowboy and his work and the words he uses. If you think you know all that then I still think you need to read these pages. For there's no one knows all about cattle and the range country. The best old cowmen will tell you that, so you'd better read it. There are some stories in it too.

ABOUT COWBOYS

WHEN KIP AND SCOOTIE came for the summer on Five barb outfit it was quite a piece of work for Uncle Bill to answer all the questions they could ask.

Uncle Bill was the name the old cowboy was known by in that country, but he had no relatives anybody knew of. As an all around rough and reckless good cowboy there were few could have tied with him some years before. Now while riding for the Five Barb outfit he was as valuable in his knowledge of range and handling cattle as any two riders could be.

"Uncle Bill," said Scootie, "how did the name cowboy come?"

Uncle Bill looked down at her and smiled.

"The name cowboy came before cowpuncher and was first fastened onto kids who used to watch over little bunches of gentle cattle so they wouldn't stray away and mix with the wild cattle. That was before range cattle were worth anything. When a railroad was built towards the West the wild cattle got to be worth some money. Not only for the hides but for the meat too. The little cowboys who'd been riding barefooted and herding their dad's gentle cattle had now grown up, and the name 'cowboy' stuck on them as they went to gathering, trailing and shipping big herds of cattle. That was the start of the American cowboy."

"But a cowpuncher—what's that?" asked Scootie, "what do you have to punch cows for?"

"I guess I'll have to explain things a bit," grinned Uncle Bill.

"When we say punching cows we mean all the works that goes on with handling cattle, like rounding 'em up, branding, herding, trail driving and all that's done with the raising, caring and shipping of 'em. It takes in all the work a cowboy or cowpuncher does. The word cowpuncher was first fastened onto fellows who worked in the stock yards when the first shipments of wild cattle was made from Texas. That was about the time when your granddad was born. The stock yard fellows used sticks and punched the cattle through the loading chutes into the cars and that's where the name cowpuncher first came in. Some of the young fellows went to riding on the range afterwards and the name stuck to 'em and sort of spread through the cow country."

"There's more I want to know about cowboys," said Scootie. "Why does a cowboy wear a big hat—and chaps, and spurs—and high-heeled boots?"

"One at a time!" said Uncle Bill. "Cowboys don't wear as big hats now as they used to. But the big hat isn't just for looks. The cowboy has a lot of use for it. On his head the brim protects his eyes from the glare of the sun and keeps it from scorching his neck. Bending his head towards a blizzard it protects him from the stinging snow. Sometimes he waves it in his hand to turn a wild horse, and he uses it for balance when he's riding a bucking horse. A cowboy is proud of his hat, but he'll use if for every need.

"Chaps, pronounced shaps, is short for chaparejos, and is sometimes called legging, for the 'shotgun' shap, which is closed or sewed on the sides.

"The most popular shap is the 'batwing,' with flaps extending from four to eight inches from the leg. These are not sewed together but fasten with two or four snaps.

"Then there's the angora goat or bearskin shap. These are either in the shotgun or batwing styles.

"Shaps are for protection from the heat as well as the cold, and the leather ones are very necessary in the prickly and spear brush that's very thick and is gone through in

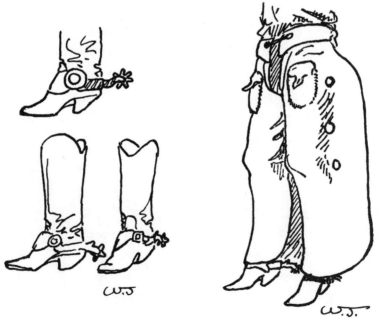

Boots, Spurs and Chaps

some southern states. Shaps are a protection and help in many other ways with the cowboy's work, more so than with the blacksmith's necessary leather apron. They're not for show and are very plain. It's only in circuses or movies that gaudy ones are seen.

"Then the high heels. Some folks think the cowboy wears them for style and good looks. But the high-heeled boots help the cowboy to do whatever his work calls for. The tops of them protect his leg from the rubbing of stirrup leather. The narrow toe fits the stirrup. The high heel keeps him from the danger of having his foot slip through the stirrup and hang. Then too, the heel will give the cowboy a sure and quick footing on any kind of ground as soon as he needs it. Lots of times he has to dodge a flying hoof in handling or saddling a horse and at such times he sure can't afford to slip."

"And don't forget the spurs," said Scootie.

"Oh, the hooks," said Uncle Bill. "We need 'em a lot. Most good rope horses are apt to check up too soon when they see the line sail towards a critter's horns. They want to brace themselves for a jerk and stopping too soon that way has spoiled many a good catch. A little touch of the spur at such a time does the work. Even the wisest and fastest horse needs the spur as a reminder once in a while."

"But isn't it cruel?" asked Scootie.

Uncle Bill frowned. "A true cowboy takes pride in being good to his horse and if spurs were unnecessary and cruel he'd never wear them. I've never seen a real cowboy cut a horse with his spurs. When he buys a pair of spurs the first thing he generally does is to file the sharp points off the rowels, so they can't cut."

ABOUT ROPING

KIP WAS TRYING to rope a corral post. He'd been trying hard and with no luck so far. The loop wouldn't stay open and he had better luck catching himself with it than he did the post.

Uncle Bill grinned as he watched him.

"How do you throw a rope, anyhow, Uncle Bill?" asked Scootie.

"Just throw it, that's all. The only thing is it takes practice, and knack too. Like learning how to play a fiddle, some folks can never learn how to play one and others can pick it up right quick."

The old cowboy took one of the ropes, made a loop, gave it a flip and made a neat catch.

"Gee, that looks easy," said Kip. "But I don't think I'll ever be able to rope like that."

"You can't tell yet. Wait till you're here awhile."

Kip and Scootie had lessons in roping from Uncle Bill. First he showed them how to tie a honda*. The binding knot is easy to tie, but the kids didn't learn to tie it, not that day.

"Now," said Uncle Bill, "don't forget you're not throwing a stick or a stone when you throw a rope. You've got to get the balance of your loop first whether you have it on or off

---

* A honda is a knot leaving enough opening for a rope to slide through.

the ground. If it's on the ground don't jerk it, just sort of drag it off a bit till you get it in the air and till you get the swing of it. The honda ought to be away from your hand and halfway down the loop to give it a good balance.

"There's about a hundred different kinds of throws," he went on. "Most every cowboy knows at least twenty-five of 'em. It all depends whether you're afoot or on horseback, standing or running, just what throw you're going to use, just like when you eat soup or meat you use a spoon for the soup and a knife for the meat."

He showed them a dozen different throws, three or four of them for catching horses in a corral and a few others for catching horses and cattle on the range. He showed them that famous throw the "Johnnie Blocker," where the loop sails out in front of a critter and then doubles back. Then he showed them the "figure eight," a mighty hard throw to make. It's used in calf roping and the loop catches the animal by the neck and front feet and crosses under the neck. He showed a few heel

You've got to get the balance of your loop first.

57

throws (hind legs) and front footing (catching horses by the front feet) and all the while the kids stood a staring in wonder.

"You don't have to whirl a loop over your head to catch anything," he said, "not unless you're riding at full speed, then you do it because your rope needs more speed than you're making yourself. But while you're in a corral, riding slow or standing still, it's best not to whirl your loop. Some outfits won't allow it, specially when catching horses, because the whirling loop scares them and makes them run around too much."

The kids kept on practicing, always remembering what Uncle Bill told them, never to rope a person, for the rope might leave a burn. One day they came to the calf pen. A few gentle calves were kept in it and the sight of them invited the kids to rope practice. They'd practiced roping the calves before but always when Uncle Bill was around. This time they were alone and they got more reckless in their roping.

There had been a heavy shower the day before. The calf pen was a little muddy and in a low place was a pool of sticky black mud. The kids stayed on the driest ground and started roping. They were getting pretty good with a rope now and they could catch a calf by the neck once in every five throws or so. The calves, being gentle, could be walked up to after each catch, and the rope taken off.

The roping went on for a spell and when they got a little tired of that they got to wondering what else to do. That's how come they thought of riding the calves after roping them. Kip caught one little fellow, got on it and had the time of his life staying on as the calf bucked around the corral. That was a lot of fun. Scootie roped and rode one too and

They were getting pretty good with a rope now.

then she caught the second calf before Kip did his. This second calf was a little bigger and not so gentle as the others, and Kip warned her that she'd have to do some hard riding on that one.

And she did have to do some hard riding. It didn't last long, just long enough for the calf to duck and head across the corral for the pool of mud. It looked as if the calf had figured on that muddy hole to teach the kids to leave him alone. Anyway he bucked in a straight line until he came to the pool, and quick as a flash, he made another buck jump right by the side of it, turned and sent Scootie scooting her whole length into the pool.

Kip about choked laughing at seeing her splash in the pool and then seeing her scramble out of it on all fours. She was green-black mud from head to foot and couldn't have been better covered with it if she'd wallowed in the pool on purpose.

She made quite a sight as she came out of the pool and stood up and started to wipe her face with her muddy hands. As soon as she got the mud out of her eyes and saw Kip laughing she got a little peeved. Then she made him do his laughing on the run for she did her best to catch him and give him a taste of a splash in the muddy hole.

But Kip wasn't weighted down with mud and he kept out of her reach. So, giving up catching him, she went to the creek to wash up as best she could. Then she went to the house where Martha gave her a good bath and a whole change of clothes, even to boots, for they were filled with mud too. By the time Uncle Bill came back she was all cleaned up, and it seemed as if nothing unusual had happened. Kip didn't tell because there was the time he had fallen off his horse, and Scootie hadn't told on *him*.

ABOUT BRANDING

THE DAY THAT KIP AND SCOOTIE saw the calves branded they had more questions. When they all got to where the herd was being held, a fire had been started a little way from the herd. While the many branding irons were heating a few ropers quietly rode through the herd to spot what belonged to their outfit. A ring of about fifteen riders was around the herd to keep the cattle from breaking out or scattering. All was done quietly so the calves did not get separated from their mammies. Each calf had to be with its mammy before it was roped and branded, so the boys would know what outfit it belonged to.

Kip and Scootie didn't see everything as the first calf was roped, brought in, ear-marked and branded. There was too much going on all at once. But as calf after calf was brought in Scootie finally managed to ask a question.

"Goodness, Uncle Bill," she said, "that branding certainly must hurt them."

"Well," said the old cowboy, "I don't guess it feels very good, but they're more scared than hurt. It's over in less than a minute anyway and I don't think it hurts any worse than having a tooth pulled."

"But what about afterwards, doesn't the burn keep on hurting?"

"I guess it does a little, but they sure don't seem to lose any sleep or fat over it."

That seemed to satisfy her for awhile and she went on watching and smelling the smoke of the burning hair. Then Kip asked, "What do they cut pieces off their ears for?"

"That's what we call ear-marking. And so we can tell whose cattle they are at a distance and without having to ride close and look at the brand."

"But isn't there some other way of marking the cattle without having to brand them?"

"None that would stick and couldn't be changed. Even some of the brands have been changed by cattle rustlers."

As Uncle Bill talked he kept a little book and pencil in his hands. As each roper brought in a calf to be branded he shouted out its mother's brand and Uncle Bill added a mark in his tally book under the brand. That was to keep track of how many cattle belonged to each owner.

There were many brands in the little tally book and as Kip got to glancing at it once in a while he wondered what the names of them were. Finally he had to ask.

"There's thousands of different kinds of brands," said the old cowboy. "The most of 'em are easy enough to read. In reading 'em you always start from the top and left, for instance. That reads 'Bar two U.' This one M seven bar. Straight letter or figure brands are easy to read, but the 'character brands' are hard even for a cowboy. They have to be known. Take 'Walking X,' that's a letter and character brand mixed and a stranger cowboy could just as well call it Double L or he might call the 'Long X,' Double L, or the 'Diamond A,' A.M. Then there are character brands such as 'Mill iron,' , 'Turkey track' and the like. You've pretty well got to hear them named before you can be sure of them."

Here are some more of the brands that Kip and Scootie found in Uncle Bill's book. See if you can read them. The right names are in the back of the book.

KIP AND SCOOTIE
HAVE AN ADVENTURE

A YEAR LATER, when Kip and Scootie came back for another summer at the ranch, they had an adventure.

The kids were riding along one day when Kip spotted what looked like a small dugout of cedar and rock half way down the ridge. This stirred Scootie's curiosity, for the dugout looked deserted and might prove to be an interesting place to explore.

A band of antelope, looking more like ghosts against formations and country of their own color, stood stock still at less than five hundred yards away and watched the kids ride by. Lizards scampered here and there and one lively rattlesnake crawled into a hole before Kip could get off his horse and head it with rocks.

As Kip and Scootie guessed, the dugout was deserted. It didn't look as though it had ever had a door, just an opening which had most likely been covered with canvas during storms.

The kids got off their horses, tied them well, and Kip took the lead from the bright sunlight into the dark opening. It was a little while before they could see inside, and at first there wasn't much to see. There was a smoked corner where the fire had been built, the opening or door being the only way for the smoke to get out. Holes had been hewed out of the sandstone for shelves, and looking up at the roof it didn't seem very safe to be under, for the timbers were close to breaking under the weight of the dirt on top. There'd been cedar boughs and bunk frame below and in one corner, but with the many bones that near covered the floor it was hard to make out. The bones were from almost every kind of animal that roamed that country, from pack rats to deer. It looked as if the animals had either come there for shelter or been dragged in by little and big cats, lynxes to lions, to feast upon or feed their young.

By all appearances the dugout hadn't been used by human beings for some years. Getting used to the dark, the kids then noticed a darker hole yawning at the back and leading into the hillside. Kip went closer, lit a match and saw it was a tunnel. A few rusted prospector's tools were still there, and with only the light of a match there was no telling how deep the tunnel was. That tunnel accounted for the ore dump they'd noticed in the front of the dugout, and whoever dug the tunnel lived at the entrance, in the dugout. The ore had been wheeled or packed through it to be dumped down the hill in front.

Must have been valuable ore, thought the kids, for the prospector to live at the entrance of his tunnel the way he did. That tunnel would need exploring, they figured. It would be fun.

But there would have to be light, and the only way to get it was to build a fire inside or at the mouth of the tunnel. That would take away the damp dead smell. They came outside, gathered some sage brush and dry cedar limbs and then going inside again with each a good armful they set part of it to burning a little way inside the tunnel.

65

The light was good but it didn't reach to the end of the tunnel, only far enough to disturb what seemed to be hundreds of bats which began flying around close by the kids' ears and almost scared them out of their wits. Scootie clamped her hat down tight and they squatted close to the floor of the tunnel, their hearts beating fit to burst,—but they weren't going to quit now and let little bats scare them out. They remembered Uncle Bill telling them how it wasn't true that bats got their claws into people's hair and the hair had to be cut off to get them loose, also it wasn't true that bats are blind, for as Uncle Bill said they could see very well, night or day. They wished he was with them now, for they wouldn't feel so spooky in exploring the tunnel.

The bats seemed to settle down from their first confusion of the light, and the kids got up enough nerve to go a little farther in the tunnel, as far as the light of their fire would reach. There they would start another fire to light them on still farther. But Kip just struck a match to the dry brush he'd carried and no more than got it into a blaze when he dropped his match and blazing brush. There'd come a low and dangerous sounding growl, and looking into the dark depth of the tunnel he saw a pair of bright yellow eyes shining from the reflection of the fire.

Scootie, of course, heard the threatening growl and seen the eyes at the very same time Kip did, but she was quicker than Kip in deciding to get away from there and back to the entrance. There was no crawling nor minding of the bats as the two went now, they were up and going fast as they could, Scootie an arm's length in the lead.

When Kip and Scootie came back to the ranch

In their fright and with the speed they were going their steps were much heavier than when they'd been crawling. They were plum careless, and when Scootie made one step while halfway to the entrance there was a sound of giving away timber and she went down suddenly out of sight. Kip, being a few feet back of her, barely managed to keep his balance but that was for only a second. There was a roar and a snarl which sounded, echoed and resounded many times louder than it was, and that took away what little balance Kip had left. Down he went the way Scootie had.

As good luck would have it, the fall wasn't deep, and then again he didn't land on Scootie. It was a mighty scary happening, this screeching wild animal, whatever it was, and then this sudden dropping into space in the darkness.

Both kids sat where they fell, close to one another and stiff with fear. Finally, not hearing any more of the wild animal's growls, Kip slowly reached in his pocket for a match and lit it, lit it just in time to look up and see a long tannish form leaping across the opening of the shaft. The match went out as quickly as it had flared up.

More shaky silence for a spell and then Kip spoke in a scared whisper, "Gee, Scootie, did you see what I did?"

Scootie whispered back that she had, and she didn't have to add that she was scared.

"It's a mountain lion," Kip whispered on, "and I'll bet he's ten feet long."

Hearing Kip's whispering nerved Scootie to speak up a little and ask, "What shall we do?"

"Why, get out of here, of course, if we can."

*Kip looked up and saw a long tannish form
leaping across the opening of the shaft.*

"But, but what about the lion?" said Scootie. "I'm so afraid . . . . Don't you think we'd better wait until Uncle Bill or Chuck comes to look for us? We're safe from the lion here, I think."

The flickering light of the small fires went dim and then dark come against the tunnel's ceiling, and Kip and Scootie went on thinking about their chances of getting away without meeting the lion. They knew the lion had leaped for the outside, but he might have come back and still be in the tunnel. Or there might be more lions, maybe a female with a litter of young ones.

Such creatures would be mighty dangerous to meet up with in a den or any narrow place, Uncle Bill had said. He's said, too, that a lion would always try to get away if possible and would never attack a human unless cornered, or unless the human came up to it in too close quarters. The tunnel would be mighty close quarters to have to pass one in, the kids thought.

With the still darkness the kids got restless and nervous. It was easy for them to imagine a lion glaring down at them and ready to pounce any moment. Then, to sort of break the spell, Kip lit another match to see about the depth and size of the shaft and for possible chances of getting out, also to make sure that no snarling lion's head was looking down at them.

It seemed to be about ten feet to the top of the shaft, and if Kip and Scootie could manage to climb up on the other's shoulders and stand, that first one could maybe get a hold so as to get out. Then the other could be helped up by the first one letting down a line of knotted clothing, belt and such.

But the thought of lion or lions made them ponder on some more, and as they got to thinking of waiting where they were till they were rescued it would be quite a long wait. They wouldn't be missed, they figured, until Chuck came in to corral the bulls for the night, it would be about dark by then and it would be impossible for their trail to be found or followed. They would have to stay in the shaft the rest of the day, the whole long night and part of the next day before they could expect any one to come to their rescue.

A long and dreadful wait, but the fear of the lion halfways decided them to try it. At least they weren't in any hurry in trying to get out, that is, not until Kip lit another match to see what his hand had come in contact with while squirming around. It felt like loose joints of a bracelet or necklace in the hard rock. The light of the match showed it was loose joints, sure enough, but not of a bracelet. It was the bones of a human hand.

A shiver went up his spine and at the same time, Scootie let out a scream, for one of her hands had been resting on what she thought was a round rock, which really was a human skull.

Well, with all the other bones that went to make up the long gone human, all white and showing up spooky in the light, that was enough to near make the kids fly up out of the shaft. Awful thoughts came to them as they stood up against a corner of the shaft and Kip lit match after match to see what all was before them. They thought maybe that lions had got the poor unfortunate whose bones they was staring at, or maybe snakes, and the same fate would be theirs if they stayed.

Right then they decided they wouldn't be staying, but being excited couldn't get anywhere in figuring out ways of getting out. They were kind of wild, like two mice swimming around in a half-filled bucket of water.

Finally cooling down some, Kip lighting another match figured it out with Scootie that if he stood against the wall and she climbed on his shoulders, she could reach one of the timbers that still held above the opening. Then if he boosted her up all he could and gave her a footing with his hands she could get up over the edge.

71

That was the only way. But Scootie thought of the lion again, and being the first one to go up didn't appeal to her. In her excitement she didn't stop to think of what trouble she'd be in if Kip went up first and she was left alone in the shaft—her bones would in time belong with those of the prospector.

Noticing her hesitating to go up, Kip was quick to say that he would. Scootie was kind of shaky, but bracing herself up against the wall, Kip made it to scramble up on her shoulders, then also steadying himself against the wall he felt for a timber that would hold his weight for the rest of the way up. A small slide of gravel and sand came down as he felt for one, and telling Scootie to keep her face down and keep standing he groped on in the dark till he found a timber he figured would hold. His high-heeled boots dug into Scootie's shoulders but she stood up under that, and when she felt a relief of Kip's weight and was told to put her hands under his feet and hold 'em up against the wall she was glad to do that. She hardly minding the extra dirt that kept a sliding, and now she'd almost forgotten about the lion.

Finally, with Kip's hard scrambling and Scootie's steady boosting him, with new toe holds he got his shoulders and then his body over the edge of the shaft, then he was up on top.

There was no lingering from there on. Stripping off his shirt and wide belt he tied the two together and told Scootie to add her shirt onto it. This made a rope that held and gave Kip a chance to get back from the shaft opening to where he could brace himself, hold on and pull.

It was no easy climbing for Scootie, but being desperate as she was to get out of the shaft, especially now that Kip

*Kip and Scootie took one
last look behind them.*

was out she had more than ordinary strength, and soon enough her head was above the opening. More scrambling and then she was alongside of Kip.

Neither paused for a breath, for as soon as Scootie got on her feet, a low echoing growl from the dark end of the tunnel put her and Kip on a tight run for the other end and sunlight. They were now sure there were two lions and they didn't dare think of meeting the one they'd seen leaping over the shaft. So they just went for all they were worth for the light and opening of the tunnel.

73

The way the kids ran it would be doubtful if a lion would of tried to catch up with them. Anyhow, there was none behind them as they come out of the tunnel and none before them as they sort of dived into the dugout and out through the opening, into the sunlight. Then they didn't slow up or look either side till they got to their horses, which meant safety.

Feeling very satisfied that they'd had enough exploring for a while, Kip and Scootie took one last look behind them as they topped a high ridge and then headed their horses back for camp. They came to a small spring on the way, drank, and watered their horses. Then, faces washed, they dusted the dirt off their clothes with their hats, and when they rode into camp late that afternoon, neither looked much the worse for their experience, only some wiser.

It was good to see old Uncle Bill there by camp as they rode in, all contented-like and puttering around the fire. The sight of him gave them a sense of security and they figured that whenever they did any more exploring it would be with him if possible, for it seemed as if they always got into more adventure than they wanted and which they wouldn't get into if the old cowboy was with them. If they did get into some adventure with him it didn't seem scary, only all the more interesting.

There was a grinning nod from him as the kids came into camp after unsaddling and hobbling their horses on good grass.

"Thought you two was on dayherd with Chuck this afternoon," he said. "Wasn't he good company?"

"We didn't go see Chuck," said Scootie. She smiled: "We went exploring."

Then she went on to tell of their adventure at the dugout, the tunnel, their fall into the shaft, the lions and the skeleton. Kip chipped in a word once in awhile, and when they got through, Uncle Bill remarked that it was quite some adventure they had, and how he'd liked to have been with them.

"Yes," says Kip. "We sure wished you'd been with us too."

Kip had pulled off one boot while speaking. Something had got in there which hurt his foot and now as he got it out he was examining a little yellow pebble which he'd found. He examined it for a while and then handed it to Uncle Bill, asking what it was.

The old cowboy took it and at a glance he saw that it was gold, a gold nugget. Kip was quite surprised and excited at that, so was Scootie, but both were more surprised that Uncle Bill wasn't at all excited and looked at the nugget as if it were a plain rock pebble. He hadn't showed much interest either when told about the skeleton in the bottom of the shaft and the place where it was most likely the nugget had worked into Kip's boot top while squirming around in there.

The kids were disappointed that Uncle Bill didn't rear up at their story and want to investigate but Uncle Bill wasn't much for treasure hunting, or digging up skeletons' pasts. He would have liked to have been with them that day but he didn't much care to make any special trip there. He was no prospector, and like most cowboys, he'd ride all his life, sometimes right by or over mineral veins that might be worth millions of dollars or a lifetime's wages, and never notice or get off his horse to hunt for gold. He'd hardly know mineral if he saw it and if he did that would only mean hard digging with pick and shovel to him and the hanging up of his saddle. That's why the lack of interest. Another thing was that no prospector was any better off than any cowpuncher, and if the prospector struck it rich in minerals the cowpuncher can also strike it the same in cattle.

With the kids' story, Uncle Bill had it summed up as to the abandoned prospect. It was a place where cattle used to go to water. The skeleton in the shaft was most likely that of the prospector who'd dug it, and the covering of the opening went to prove pretty well that he'd been killed for what gold he'd got and then thrown in there. If he'd died by accident it wouldn't be likely that he'd been left there when found. The shaft opening was easy to cover up, along with traces of the crime, and as the timbers were so rotted so as not to hold the kids' weight this showed that the crime had been committed too many years past for the facts to be dug up.

"And as for gold," Uncle Bill went on to say, "if any more of it was there the one or ones who covered up the shaft would have been sure to've got it. It would only be pocket gold anyway and the finding of it would be just pure luck. There's no gold veins in this part of the country that I know of, nor any worth while deposits. If there was, somebody would sure have known about it.

"For my part, I wouldn't raise a sweat about it nor disturb the skeleton that's been resting there so long. Of course, with some young fellow like Chuck, if you mention gold to him his ears might perk up some and maybe he'd get to investigating it during some winter months when there's not so much riding. But I'll bet if he got the lions he'd make more money out of their hides and bounty on 'em than all the gold he'd ever find there."

So that was that, and how the kids went lion hunting is another story.

It was a place where cattle used to go to water.

UNCLE BILL
TELLS A STORY

THERE WAS SELDOM a noon hour when the old cowboy didn't tell of some of his experiences while camping in different parts of the range country. He'd seen many parts of it before he settled down to riding for the Five-Barb, parts where it got to sixty below zero in winters, and other parts to the south where it was sixty above zero at the same time of the year. His rambling trail had covered thousands of miles of range land. He'd camped alongside of snowdrifts, and other times when canyons were like red hot furnaces. As he went to telling of his experiences, it was in a way that'd be a sort of teaching to the kids so that no matter where they camped they'd get an idea of what to do, how and when to travel, how to go by signs on land and sky, and how to take care of themselves and their horses.

"I stopped by a big dry washout one time," said Uncle Bill. "It was in the big desert a long ways south of here. I'd been following that wash thinking I'd find some little pool of water in some of the hollowed rocks that were in the bottom of it. I was so dry that I'd have chewed mud if I'd found some. My horse was ganted up and just as dry as I was and he wouldn't even put his head down to look for grass. He wasn't hungry, and it was just as well he wasn't because there was nothing for him to eat anyhow, nothing but little black twisted-up sage.

"In the back of my saddle I had some 'jerky' (dried beef or venison) and soda crackers, the best things to take when a man is travelling across country without a pack horse. It's light, and four or five pounds of that together will keep a cowboy in good shape for a week or more. But I didn't touch any of the jerky or crackers, because I wasn't hungry either.

"The more thirsty you are the less appetite you have, and even tho we'd been drifting steadily, my horse and I were at the stage where we didn't have any appetite at all, for neither of us had touched moisture for about two days. I'd kept moving a little pebble in my mouth to sort of keep what saliva I had left in me circulating and I didn't take the bridle off my horse because the bit in his mouth helped him the same way as the pebble did me."

"Well, to go on with the story, I didn't stop by the dry wash to eat, it was to rest while the heat was at its worst and to save what strength the horse and I had for when it got cooler. There's one thing about the old desert. It may sizzle you during the day but it usually makes you wear a coat or reach for a blanket during the night.

"My horse went to sleep standing and I sort of dozed in the shade of him, but I didn't dare doze hard nor take on too much of the shade he made, because he was weaving like a willow to a breeze, and I was afraid he might fall on me. I'd come out of my dozes suddenly every once in a while and blink at the long distances of flat white and sizzling landscape all around me. Outside of far away low and dry hills there wasn't a break in the whole land but the dry wash

I was alongside of. I figured on hitting for the dry hills soon as it begin to get cooler, and I was hoping that I would run across some trail on the way, some trail made by hoofs of antelope or wild horse, because then I'd know there'd be water in those hills and all I'd have to do is follow the trail to wherever it was."

Here Scootie interrupted with a question. "Didn't you have a canteen of water along with you?" she asked.

"No. I've never seen a cowboy pack a canteen on his saddle. It flops too much and he figures it an awkward and unnecessary weight. He'll laugh at anybody who packs one and class him as a tenderfoot. Another thing is the feeling every good cowboy has for his horse. If he can't take along enough for the horse, he'll go without it too, and save him that extra weight. It's only when he has a pack horse along that he might add on a canteen if the pack is light, but seldom even then.

"The desert rider is used to going a long time without water, or without anything to eat, and if he's pretty sure of striking a camp where he'll get grub within twenty-four hours, he won't take even a bite along. It's only when going on a many days' ride that he'll take anything to eat, and then he'll most likely have a pack horse and take his bedding along too. I've heard tell of cowboys sleeping in their saddle blankets, that's true enough and most every cowboy has had to often enough, but that goes better in a story than it does in life. If he can, the cowboy will have his tarpaulin covered bedding to crawl into when comes his chance to rest.

"It's only when he's in a heap of a hurry that he'll leave his pack horse behind, and then, if he's going on a long trip, he'll just roll up a half dozen pounds of jerky and biscuits or bannock mixed and tie it on his saddle. He won't take a flopping canteen, not even tho he knows he might sometime wish that he had.

"I was mighty thirsty that day when I stopped along that dry wash, but I never thought of a canteen because I'd never packed one. Finding a hoof mark is all that was in my mind. That would be a sign there was water somewhere and maybe not too far away. It seemed a mighty long time since I'd seen a hoof mark of any kind, only when I'd doze a bit during the heat of the day, then I'd see them in my dream.

"The sun was hitting for the west and beginning to lose some of its heat when I stood up and blinked at the ocean of land around me. I stirred my tired and thirsty horse, and we both started slowly to putting one foot ahead of the other, me leading him. We must have gone about a mile, still following the wash, when I stopped short, thinking I was out of my head, for right by my boot toe was what looked like the print of an antelope's hoof in the hardpan dirt. And it was, but I had to feel of it with my fingers to make sure.

"Of course I knew that antelope often go a long ways from water, and this hoof print I saw might have been twenty miles from any, but it was encouraging to see that something alive had been where I was and had kept on going, even if it was a speedy antelope. I talked to my horse about it, tried to make him look at the dim hoof print, and wished he'd understand what the sight of it meant.

"The sight of that hoof print sure brought new life to me, and I went as crazy to looking for more as a prospector goes crazy when he finds his first flake of gold. I found more hoof prints, zigzagging all directions, which showed that the antelope had just been roaming around and headed for no particular place. But I knew that the tracks would sooner or later get in with some others and finally lead me to water if I followed them. I sure followed them, and my nose nearly touched the ground as I did because I was afraid I would lose sight of 'em. The tracks got more plentiful as I went and that was encouraging, but as I'd straighten up and look around once in a while it didn't look as if there would be water.

"Then, as I followed the antelope tracks, I got another surprise that made me rub my eyes and look a few times. It was the hoof print of a horse, and further on there were more of them. Now I knew that horses seldom go over ten or fifteen miles from water. I saw more horse tracks. I picked up speed and after a while I came to a plain trail where there were lots of horse and antelope tracks.

"The trail was easy to follow now and I didn't have to keep my nose to the ground any more, but as I looked over the country ahead, I couldn't see any sign of where there could be water to within any ten or fifteen miles, even if there were plenty of horse tracks on the trail. I got on my horse to get a little higher view, rode along for a few miles, and then I got the sudden sight of a bunch of antelope.

"At the sight of the antelope and the way they were bunched, I made my weaving horse walk a little faster, for it looked to me as if the antelope were drinking.

"It seemed to take a mighty long time to cover the distance to the antelope and to help my horse I got off him and walked some more. I was even pulling him, and the poor beast was

*I got sudden sight of
a bunch of antelope*

so all in that he didn't see the antelope that only walked
away when I got to within a few hundred yards of them.

"I can't begin to describe to you kids how I felt when,
as I looked at the closest of the antelope, I saw drops of
water dripping from their chins. In the sun the drops looked
like diamonds, and to me they looked a heap more precious
than any diamond. But where was the water hole? . . . the
land was flat, not a hollow anywhere. My heart sort of went
up my throat as I kept on walking and looking, thinking that
maybe I surely was out of my head this time. Then as I made
another step I came near walking over it, the water hole.

"It was a sure enough water hole, and I could never find out or guess how deep it was, but the top of the hole was only about the size of a horse's hoof print. Clear water was bubbling up in it in a way that reminded me of drinking fountains I've seen in towns. None of the water flowed out of the hole, just bubbled as if it were coming up for air and churned back underground. By that and the depth of the hole I figured that water to be from a big underground river, maybe a mile below.

"You can bet your boots that I didn't stop to do any figuring as to where that water came from when I first spotted it. I didn't even stop to think that it might be poisonous. If I had, the antelope were enough proof that it wasn't. There were signs that they'd been watering there regularly and I couldn't see bleached bones anywhere around. Anyhow, I scooped up a handful of that water and splashed it on my horse's nostrils, and if I ever saw a horse come out of it sudden it was him. I splashed some more over his eyes and head and then, leaving the bit in his mouth so I could hold him and so he wouldn't gulp so fast, I let him have a few sips. I had to be mighty careful not to let him have too much at once or it might have killed him.

"After I let him have his first few sips I held him back with one hand while I used the other to splash water over my own head and face. I spit out my pebble and held water in my mouth instead of it. Then I gargled some, and finally I swallowed a couple of sips myself. My tongue wasn't swelled much, but I went easy on that water just the same.

"The thirst being sort of checked up some, I led my horse away from the water so the sight of it wouldn't be too much of a temptation. I sure wasn't going to go very far, not for quite a spell. But I didn't get much farther than a hundred yards away from the water hole when I found another of the exact same kind and size. Then I looked towards the horses that were a couple of miles away and they acted as if they were drinking out of another of the natural fountains. I scooped a couple of swallows out of the second hole, let my horse have a few more sips, and then went on to where the bunch of horses was. Another water hole was there sure enough, and I thought I must have been following in line with the underground river.

"But now it looked like this hole was the last one where the underground river came to the top and I didn't get very far away from it. If there'd been any grass around for my horse, I'd have stayed there all night, but there's never any feed of any kind close to water in the desert because the stock always graze that off first, as they leave the water.

"The sun went down, the air got nice and cool and then, after taking on some more water, I began to feel normal again and my appetite soon came back. I chewed on some jerky and crackers while wishing there was something for my horse to eat, for he was fast beginning to feel normal too, and hungry enough so he nibbled at the dry sage.

"I guess it was along about midnight when I let my horse have all the water he wanted. He was hungry but he was pretty strong again. He had a good rest and lost his weaving walk. I took on all I could hold of water, got on my horse, and for the first time in my life I wished I had a canteen to take some along.

"But I wouldn't of had much need for a canteen from then on because as early morning came, after I'd crossed the low hills, I saw the dim outline of mountains against the sky, and when the sun came up to shine on them they looked good, for I saw they were covered with timber. There was quaker in the canyons and that meant water there and bunch grass on the hillsides. It was just getting good and hot again when my horse splashed ankle deep in a cool little stream which we both took a drink out of and then we went on up it into the cool shade of the quakers where I unsaddled and made camp.

"I left my horse loose up on the side of the hill where he could bury his head up to his eyes in bunch grass. He wouldn't leave because he was sure ready to make camp too."

The old cowboy had come to the end of his story and everything was quiet for a spell. Kip stared away off in the distance and then he finally said, "Gee, Uncle Bill, I wish I'd been with you!"

Horses and Their Ways

EVERY MAN who uses and really knows horses realizes that that animal is his best friend. The horse will pack him at any speed, any time or place, and work for and with his rider without a whine, no matter how hungry, thirsty or sore footed he may be.

Always remember that a horse has plenty of heart and feelings like any good friend, and treat him as such. He's not a hunk of machinery.

SMOKY,
THE RANGE COLT

The First Day

SMOKY DIDN'T SEE the first light of day through a box-stall window and there was no human around to make a fuss over him and try to steady him on his feet for the first few steps. Smoky was just a little range colt, born on the wide prairie, and all the company he had that first morning of his life was his watchful mammy.

Smoky wasn't quite an hour old when he began to take interest in things. The warm spring sun was doing its work and kept pouring warmth right through his little body. Pretty soon his head come up kind of shaky and he began nosing around his own long front legs that were stretched out in front of him. His mammy was close by him, and, at the first move the colt made, she run her nose along his short neck and nickered softly. Smoky's head went up another two inches at the sound and his first little answering nicker was heard.

That was the starting of Smoky. Pretty soon his ears began to work back and forth towards the sound his mammy would make as she moved. He was trying to find out just where she was. Then something moved right in front of his nose, it had been there all the time but his vision was a little dim yet. That something moved again and planted itself still closer. He took a sniff at it. It was one of his mammy's legs. His ears pricked up and he tried nickering again.

Then he made a sudden scramble to get up but his legs wouldn't work right. One of his front legs gave way and the whole works went down.

He lay there flat on his side, breathing hard for a spell. His mammy nickered and kept talking to him in horse language. The spring air had a lot to do to keep Smoky from lying still very long. He gathered his legs under him to try again. Then he sniffed at the ground to make sure it was there, his head went up, his front feet stretched out in front of him. He used all the strength that was in him, and pushed

Pretty soon his ears began to work back and forth.

himself up on his front feet. His hind legs straightened up to steady him and all he had to do was to keep his legs stiff and from folding up under him. This wasn't easy, for those long legs of his were new and doing a heap of shaking.

All would have been well maybe, only his mammy nickered "that's a good boy," and that queered Smoky. His head went up proud as a peacock and he forgot all about keeping his legs stiff under him. Down he went and lay there the same as before.

But he didn't stay long this time. He was up again, mighty shaky, but he was up. His mammy came to him. She sniffed at him and he sniffed back. Then he nursed, and his tummy warmed up and strength came fast. Smoky was an hour and a half old and up to stay.

Things got interesting from then on, and the rest of that day was full of events for Smoky. He explored the country and at one time was as far as twelve feet away from his mammy all by himself. He shied at a rock once; it was a dangerous *looking* rock and he kicked at it as he went past. That was almost too much for him and he come close to going down again. But luck was with him, and taking it all he had a mighty good time. When the sun sank over the blue ridges in the west that evening Smoky was stretched out, all tired out and fast asleep.

There wasn't a move out of him till the sun was well up and beginning to throw a good heat. His mammy nickered and that woke him. Smoky raised his head, looked around, and then began to get up. It was much easier this time and after a little while that was done. Smoky was ready for a new day.

Smoky and the Coyote

The big day started right after Smoky had his feed. His mother moved away towards some trees a mile or so to the south. She was longing for a drink of water, but she went slowly so that little Smoky could keep up with her. There were all kinds of things he had to find out about.

A baby cottontail jumped up once right under Smoky's nose. The cottontail stood there a second, too scared to move, and pretty soon made a high dive between the colt's long legs and hit out for his hole. Smoky never saw the rabbit or he might have been running yet, because that's what he'd been looking for, an excuse to run.

But at last he made up an excuse and as a long dry weed tickled his belly he let out a squeal and went from there.

His long legs tangled and untangled themselves as he ran, and he sure was making speed. Around and around he went and finally lined out straight away from where his mammy was headed. She nickered for him, and waited. He turned after a while and when he got close to his mammy he let out a buck, a squeal, a snort and stopped. He was sure some little wild horse.

It took a couple of hours for the two to make that mile to the spring. The mother drank a lot of the good water. Smoky came over and nosed at the pool, but he didn't take on any of the fluid. It looked like so much thin air to him.

The rest of that day was spent around that spot. There were adventures of all kinds for Smoky. Plenty of big tree stumps gave him the scare he'd be looking for.

But there were other things more dangerous than stumps that Smoky hadn't seen. A big coyote had been watching him through dead willow branches. He wasn't at all interested in Smoky's play, only wished the colt's mammy would move away. Then he would try to get him down, for colt meat was his favorite dish.

Smoky's mammy stayed too close and the coyote finally came out of his hiding place. He squatted again, in plain sight this time. He hadn't quite made up his mind whether to go or to stick around a while longer. Just about then Smoky spotted him.

To him, the coyote was just another stump, but a stump that moved. Smoky trotted up to the coyote. The coyote just sat there and waited and when the colt got to within a few feet of him he started away just fast enough so the colt would follow. If he could only get the colt over the ridge and out of his mammy's sight!

It was all a lot of fun to Smoky, and he was bound to find out what was that gray and yellow thing that could move and didn't look at all like his mammy. It wasn't till he was over the hill that he saw all wasn't well.

The coyote had turned and, quicker than a flash, made a jump for Smoky's throat. Because his father and his grandfather and his great-grandfather had fought the wolf and the coyote, Smoky knew what to do. He whirled and let fly with both hind feet. The coyote's teeth had just pinched the skin under his jaws. But even at that, Smoky wasn't going to get rid of his enemy that easy. As he kicked he felt the weight of the coyote and then a sharp pain in his hind leg.

Smoky was scared, and he let out a squeal. It was a plain and loud enough distress signal, and it was answered. His mammy shot up the hill and took in the goings-on at a glance.

Then, ears back, teeth shining, she tore up the earth and lit into the battle.

The battle was over in a second, and, with hunks of yellow fur flying, it ended in a chase. The coyote was in the lead and he stayed in the lead until a second hill took him out of sight.

Smoky was glad to follow his mammy back to the spring. A thin stream of blood was drying on one of his hind legs, but there was no pain. It was just a scratch. When the sun set and the shadow of his mammy spread out over him he was soon sound asleep again, and maybe dreaming of stumps, of stumps that moved.

His long legs tangled and untangled themselves.

Smoky and the Yellow Animal

The spring days were great for Smoky; he found out a lot of things. He found out that grass was good to eat and water mighty fine to drink when the day was hot. He saw coyotes again, and the bigger he got the less he was afraid of them. Finally, he went to chasing every one of them he'd see.

Then one day he ran across another yellow animal. That animal didn't look dangerous. What's more it was hard for Smoky to make out just what it was, and he was bound to find out. He followed that animal to the edge of some willows. The queer part of it was that the animal didn't seem at all in a hurry to get away. It was just taking its time and Smoky was mighty tempted to paw it. As luck would have it he didn't have the chance, the animal got in under some willows and all that was sticking out was part of its tail. Smoky took a sniff at the tail. There didn't seem to be any danger, so the next sniff he took was a little closer. That did the trick. Smoky let out a squeal and a snort as the four-inch porcupine quills went into his nostrils.

But Smoky was lucky, for, if he'd been a couple of inches closer, the quills would have been rammed into his nose up to his eyes. As it was, there were just a few quills in his nostrils, and, compared to the real dose he might have got, it was just a warning to him. Another lesson.

More Lessons

It was in one of his wild scrambles down a mountain side that Smoky almost ran into a cinnamon bear cub. It had been curled up and sleeping on top of a big stump. Smoky stood still in his tracks for a second, and in that second the cub fell off the stump with a snarl and started the other side.

Smoky went after it. Over dead timber he went, and ducked under branches. He was gaining, but, just when things were getting real interesting, there was a crash and something that sounded like a landslide. In half a second more a big round head showed itself through the underbrush. Smoky saw two small eyes afire, long white teeth gleaming, and when he heard a roar that shook the mountains, Smoky left. He tore a hole in the earth as he turned tail, and raced back towards his mammy and safety.

His heart was thumping fit to burst as he got out in open country. For the life of him he couldn't figure out how that little bunch of fur he'd been chasing could turn out into such a cyclone. He'd never reckoned the little cub had a mammy, too.

But Smoky was learning fast. Another time on the foothills his mammy was in the lead and he was following close behind on a hot dusty trail. Of a sudden there was a rattling sound, and his mammy left the trail as though she'd been shot. Smoky did the same and none too soon. On the left, just a foot or so off the trail was a wriggling thing that had struck and missed his ankle by an inch.

Smoky stood off at a safe distance and snorted at the snake as it coiled up, ready. Somehow he had no hankering to sniff at the gray and dirty colored rattler, and when his mammy nickered for him to follow there was a warning in her nicker. He took another look at the snake. He would remember, and do the same as his mother had done whenever the rattling sound would be heard again.

The little horse was having a great time up there in that high country. He never passed anything that had him wondering. If a limb cracked within hearing distance he'd perk his ears towards the sound and seldom would go on until he'd found out just why that limb cracked that way. He'd follow and pester the badger until it would hunt a hole; he'd circle around a tree and watch the bushy-tailed squirrel as it would climb up out of his reach. Skunks had crossed his trail, too, but something about them made him keep his distance.

Smoky had met all the range country's wild animals but the lion and the wolf. His mammy kept clear of the places where these outlaws ranged. Smoky met them and had scrambles with them, but that came later in his life. It's a good thing it was later, or most likely I wouldn't be telling about Smoky now

Smoky and the Human

The first big event of Smoky's life came when he was four months old. He was standing up and asleep. His mammy was asleep too, so were the rest of the bunch. When the cowboy that was riding up the canyon spotted them he knew he could get above them and be where he could start them down before any of the bunch would see him.

It was a mighty good thing he done that, for, as soon as one of the bunch got wind of him, there was a snort, they came to life and were on the run. Down the side of the canyon they went, a cloud of dust and the cowboy following.

Deep and far-apart tracks were made in the steep earth as the horses slid off the mountain, jumped off ledges and sailed acrost washouts. It was away out on the flat that Smoky looked back and got his first sight of the human. The way his mammy and the bunch acted made Smoky know that here was a different kind of animal, the kind that no horse would stop to fight but run away from, if it was possible.

But it didn't seem possible, for the rider was still right close after them. He stayed close till he drove the bunch into the big log corrals. The corrals seemed to Smoky like trees growing sideways instead of up and down. But the little horse knew that there was no going through those trees. He stuck close as he could to his mammy's side. She and the bunch milled around the big pen and the big gate closed on them.

Wild eyed, the bunch turned and faced a bow legged, leather-covered, sunburnt human.

Smoky shivered as he watched that strange creature get off a horse just like the others in the bunch except for a funny hunk of leather on his back. Pretty soon the human fumbled around a while and that hunk of leather was pulled off. The horse shook himself and walked towards Smoky and the bunch.

The colt never missed a thing. As soon as the loose horse came his way he took a sniff at his sweaty hide to see just what had been sitting on him all through that long run. The sniff left him more puzzled than ever and he looked again at the creature that was standing up on two legs.

There had been a lot of lightning up in the mountains and Smoky had seen some fires there too. The lightning and the fires were great puzzles to the colt. So when he saw the human make a swift move with a paw, and then saw a fire in that paw, and then smoke coming out of the mouth, it

97

made things all the harder for him to figure out. He stood and watched.

Pretty soon, the same paws that had held the fire reached down and picked up a coil of rope, a loop was made, and the human walked towards him and the bunch. At that move the bunch tore around the corral and raised the dust.

Then Smoky heard the hiss of a rope as it sailed over past him and the loop settled on one of the ponies' heads. The pony was stopped and led out to the hunk of leather on the ground and it was put on him as it had been on the other horse. The human climbed on and that was when Smoky first set eyes on one of his kind in a fight with a two-legged creature.

It was a great sight to the colt. He watched with blazing eyes through the fight, until the pony's hard jumps became only crow-hops, then stopped. He watched the man as he got off the horse, opened the gate and led the horse out. After closing the gate he rode on and out of sight.

The Smoky rubbed noses with his mammy and went to sniffing around the big corral. After a time he noticed a dust, and with that dust came half a dozen riders. The sight of them made Smoky hurry to his mammy's side. Once there he took in all that could be seen again and watched the riders drive their horses through the gate and turn them in with his bunch. There was a lot of dust and milling around for there were now nearly two hundred horses in the big corral.

Smoky kept hidden as well as he could and watched through the horses' legs or through any opening there might be. He saw on the outside, close to the pen, a fire started.

One of his kind in a fight with the two-legged creature

Long bars of iron were passed through between the logs, with one end of them in the hot blaze.

Now many of the horses were cut out into another big corral, till there were only about fifty left. These were mostly colts about Smoky's age, and a few quiet old mares.

Smoky had no chance to hide. He saw the bow-legged humans uncoil long ropes and heard the loops whiz past him. Terror struck in his heart and he was ready to leave the earth. It was during one of his wild scrambles for a get-away that Smoky heard the close hiss of a rope, and something like a snake coiled itself around his front legs. He let out a squeal and in another second he was flat to the ground with three of his feet tied up.

Smoky figured the end of the world had come as he felt the human touch him. He cringed and quivered but he was helpless. He saw one of the creatures run towards him with a hot iron, smelled burning hair and hide. It was his own that burned but it felt cool and there was no pain for he was at the stage where the branding iron was no worse than the touch from the human hand. But there's an end to all, whether it's good or bad, and, pretty soon Smoky felt the ropes come off his legs and a boost to let him know that all was over. When he stood up and ran back to the bunch there was a mark on his hide that was there for life, the brand read R . The little horse belonged to the Rocking R outfit.

It was all a great relief to Smoky and the other colts when the branding came to an end. Then the colts found their mammies and all were turned out free again, free to go back to the high mountain ranges or run on the flats.

TOM AND JERRY

I'VE OFTEN SEEN PONIES PAIR OFF, form a partnership and stick by themselves, and they'd fight for one another when there was a need to.

That's the kind of partners Tom and Jerry were. Maybe it was because they were full brothers but anyway they were sure *for* one another. By their color and markings and size you could hardly

Tom and Jerry were partners.

tell them apart. Both were blood bays with one white hind foot and a star in the forehead. And in the way they acted they were alike, too.

I paid twenty dollars for them when they were two-year-olds. Tom was four and Jerry was five when I started breaking them in. I found them both wiry and full of snorts, and between the two of them I got many a good shaking up. But when I got through with them I had two more good horses to my string of private saddle horses.

I'd always noticed that when I turned them out on the range with the other horses they never seemed to want to run with any bunch. Instead they'd always go by themselves and I never failed to find them all by their lonesome, never more than a few feet apart.

But I had no idea how strong their partnership really was until one spring when I'd hunted high and low for them and couldn't find them. I'd got to thinking they'd left the country and gone back to their home range, which was more than a hundred miles away. Then one day, as I was riding along watching for them, I saw a lone horse in the bottom of a coulee. He was running around in small circles and seemed to be chasing something. I couldn't make out just what he was chasing. I was too far away to tell. The thing he was chasing would always turn around and come back to the place where that lone horse made his stand.

I kept a low ridge between me and the spot where I'd seen the lone horse and rode on to where I thought I'd be as close as I could get without being seen. Then I rode for the ridge straight to where things were happening.

I didn't ride over the ridge but just so I could see over it. I found that the lone horse was Jerry and then I saw what he was chasing. It was a big gray wolf. Right away I could see that Jerry was tired out and the wolf knew he couldn't fight much longer.

If I'd had my rifle with me I could have shot the wolf. I was too far for a sure shot with my six-shooter, but, as I got off my horse and dragged myself through the tall grass, I hoped the wolf would keep on being interested in Jerry just long enough so I could get near.

Where could Tom be, I wondered, as I eased myself towards Jerry and the wolf. Then I thought how queer Jerry was acting. Every time he'd chase the wolf away he'd come back and stand in one spot as if waiting for him to come again. If the wolf came too close the little horse would make a high dive for him with flying hoofs, ears set back and teeth showing.

Jerry was near all in, every hair on him was wet with sweat and from the way he looked I knew he hadn't had water for a couple of days or more. He hadn't eaten anything either, for a horse that's real thirsty doesn't hanker for grass.

What was it that kept him from leaving that spot and going to water? I wondered, but my wondering was cut short by the wolf. He'd got wind of me when I was about a hundred yards from him, and he threw up his head, sniffed the air and started traveling.

My forty-five spoke to him. Mister Wolf jumped in the air a good six feet and when he landed I let another shot go his way. I fired at him till my gun was empty and each shot only seemed to make him go faster. When I straightened up and watched him go over a hill I thought I saw him dragging one useless front leg.

Jerry was shaking like a leaf. The shots surprised and scared him but he was still in that one spot when I started towards him. I kept watching him to see what was the matter and the closer I got the more that little horse acted glad to see me.

He'd nicker softly, look down to one side of the spot where he'd been standing, then look at me again.

I got to him fast as I could. As soon as I got there I saw the reason why Jerry hadn't tried to get away from the wolf, why he'd got along without water or feed and why he stayed, fought, and protected that spot so long. A hole had been washed out by the snow waters and in that hole, lying on his back, feet in the air and very helpless was Tom—Jerry's partner.

I figured that Tom had been taking a roll and he'd picked a bad place for the purpose. When he rolled over he was too close to the edge of the hole and down in it he went. The more he tried to get out of the hole the more he found himself wedged in to stay.

A horse can't live very long in that unnatural position, so I didn't waste much time. I made a run for the saddle horse I'd left on the ridge, and, with my rope and his strength, I soon got Tom out and right side up.

All the time Jerry was watching me, and when I finally got Tom's feet under him, he came to him, sniffed along Tom's mane and nickered. Tom nickered back.

I couldn't do any more to help them so I just set there on the edge of the bank. I watched the two ponies and thought a lot. I noticed Jerry staggering for want of water. He'd fought hard and long to save his partner from the wolf, and now that all danger was over he was weak.

He stood there by Tom and *waited* for him to get on his feet so they could both go to the creek together—the creek was only a mile or so away. Pretty soon Tom showed signs of interest in life and tried to get on his feet. I was right there to help him all I could, and after a while Tom managed to stand on his legs. Mighty weak, of course, but sure enough standing.

After that it was just a case of waiting, then Tom took one step, then another.

Jerry watched him and when Tom showed he was going to keep on going, Jerry caught up with him. Both a-staggering, they headed down the coulee towards the creek.

"Yep," I said to myself as I watched the ponies move away—" and Tom would have done the same for Jerry, too."

Some Cowboy Adventures

IT'S QUEER HOW THINGS CAN HAPPEN when they're least expected. All of a sudden you're in a fix and you begin to count the minutes you've got left to live in. . . . It seems to me that there ought to be some sort of warning so a fellow can get ready for what's coming, or dodge it if he can.

Here are two stories of the tight places I've found myself getting into.

WILL JAMES
'30

A TIGHT SQUEEZE

O F ALL THE "TIGHT SQUEEZES" I've had there's one I specially remember. Right today when I think of it I feel a chill running up and down my backbone.

I was riding a big spooky horse on circle one morning during the spring round-up. When this horse was a colt he'd bucked into a hornet's nest and he kept bucking at every excuse since. The shadow of a bird on the ground was enough to get him started, and a hornet or a deer fly hanging around his nose was sure to make him act up. He'd strike at them and go to bucking and he didn't make things at all comfortable for the rider that was on him.

As I was going along, I saw tracks on the sandy trail going up into the Bad Lands. So I turned my horse to go after the stock that had made the tracks. As the trail got steeper, Spooks (as the horse was named) wanted to slow down, and I let him.

We went along on a dog trot and the trail kept getting narrower. We crossed a few bad spots and I noticed that Spooks was getting ticklish and "scared at his tail," meaning that he wanted to act up for no reason at all. He was getting even with me for the way I'd made him behave on flat ground. I couldn't spin him around up there on that trail, or set him where I wanted him, and he knew it.

We were up in the eagle country and it was a long way down to flat ground. It was a mighty good country for birds up there, and goats, too.

I was making myself as small as possible and keeping mighty quiet as we went up and up. I was handing pet words to that horse and at the same time wishing I had him down in decent country where I could take the kinks out of him.

But the worst was yet to come. I knew it at a glance as I looked at the trail ahead. The spring waters had washed out a big gash on the face of the cliff and it had taken six feet off the trail. Where that trail went on again on the other side, it was a few feet higher. This made it mighty hard to jump and a bronc is not much on jumping, except when he's bucking.

I saw there was nothing to do but ride on to where I had to stop, and that came soon enough. Spooks knew that this was a place where he could scare the life out of me and he did a fine job. He stood there for a minute, then snorted and shook himself and started rearing up.

There was no turning back, for there was only about two feet of trail to stand on. Both sides of us went straight up and down, for a couple of hundred feet. I think I prayed there for a while and I thought I'd better try the jump before that horse got it into his head to start flying down off our perch.

I showed him the trail as best I could and let him snort at the opening he had to jump. Just then a little hornet started buzzing and I didn't want to think what would happen if it ever got near Spook's nose. Instead I acted. I showed the horse the trail once again and then I touched him with the spur.

He let out a snort but behaved pretty well until he came to where he had to make the jump. There he stopped so quickly that the earth started going out from under him and we were starting to slide over the edge.

Somehow he caught himself and then I felt kind of weak. I never could stand height. We both stood there and shivered for a spell. When my heart slowed down again I began to see red. I was getting peeved at the thought of that fool horse getting funny at such a place.

From then on I made the horse think I had him on flat ground. That took him by surprise and when it came time to jump he never hesitated; I didn't give him time to. He stretched out like a flying squirrel and sailed over to the other side. His front feet met solid earth but his hind ones didn't have such luck.

I wasn't peeved then, I was just plain scared and my heart went up my throat. There was no foolishness left in that big horse either, right then. He worked and clawed and every time the dirt would give 'way from under one hind foot another would come up and take its place till it seemed there'd be no end to it.

The big horse was going further back and loosing ground at every lunge he'd make, and he was taking me with him. I had a good chance to jump off him right then, but that never came to my mind. I knew that my weight on his withers was all that was saving him from falling straight over backwards into nowhere.

Spooks knew that, I'm sure, and he was putting up a game fight. He was still trying when most ponies would have quit and gone down. Finally, when all hope seemed past,

*He snorted and shook himself
and started rearing up.*

the big bay
horse let out a
squeal and tore at the
earth with his hoofs until it shook all around. I felt his back
muscles working even under my saddle. Then all at once his
feet found solid earth.

We went on a way until the trail grew wider and we saw
clear sailing ahead. Then I got out of my saddle and loosened
up the cinches so as to give the horse a good chance to
breathe. Spooks didn't seem to mind when I ran my hand
along his neck.

"Little horse," I said, as I rubbed him back of the ears,
"you may be a fool, sometimes, but you've sure got spunk."

111

A NARROW ESCAPE

I WAS RIDING ALONG one day whistling a tune, my horse was behaving fine, and all was hunkydory and peaceful. I had noticed a narrow washout ahead but I kept on riding. I'd gone over many of them before and I didn't see any reason why I should go around this one.

My horse cleared the opening and I was still whistling. Then, of a sudden, my whistling stopped short. I felt the earth go out from under my horse's feet. The next thing I knew I was in the bottom of the washout with the horse on top of me.

I was there to stay and it was lucky that my whole body wasn't underneath that horse. As it was I was kind of on the side of him. My head was along his neck and only my left hip and leg felt the pinch of his weight.

The washout was only about three feet wide at the bottom, just big enough for me and the horse to get wedged in. The old pony was fighting and kicking big hunks of dirt down on top of us. I was worried that he might kick the bank of the washout until it caved in on us and buried us alive. So I grabbed his head and held it tight toward me, thinking that would quiet him down.

Well, he fought on for quite a spell, then he lay still for a while. Just as soon as I'd move he'd let out a snort and

*I'd gone over many a washout and I didn't
see why I should go around this one.*

start fighting again. The dirt kept piling on top of us till there was nothing but part of the horse's legs and our heads sticking out.

Then it came to me that if that horse kept on kicking and bringing down more dirt he'd soon be in a fix. His legs would all be buried and he'd have to be still. I sure was worried about a big hunk of dirt that was hanging over the edge of the washout and right above us. It looked as if it weighed at least five tons and I didn't want to think of it dropping down on us.

There was one way I could win out. That was to dig for my six-shooter which was on my right hip. With that six-shooter I could shoot the horse. Then there would be no more dirt coming down and I could dig myself out with the gun. I could take my time about it, too.

That was one way, and the best one, but I didn't want to shoot that horse. I kept my eye on the hunk of dirt above my head. Small piles of dirt kept coming down and I couldn't breathe so well.

I thought of the boys I'd started out from camp with that morning and I wondered *when* they'd miss me and start looking for me. Then, once again, I thought of my six-gun. If I could get it out and fire a shot maybe some of the boys would hear.

It took me a good hour to dig the gun out. Then I shook the dirt out of the barrel, held it straight up and fired. The shot echoed along the washout and sounded as if it could be heard for many miles. But the boys were too far away to hear.

I kept on digging. The sun had been shining in on us and making it hot down there but now it left us. It was going west to its setting point and it left me doing some tall thinking.

The big horse alongside of me was quiet—the dirt had piled up on him and he *had* to be still. But his breathing wasn't very good to listen to so close to my head.

As I worked and clawed at the dirt, I found I had to rest oftener. Just as the sun was going down I found I was holding in my hand a clump of rabbit brush. I studied where that piece of brush had come from. I felt a chill run up and down my backbone when I found that it had come from the big hunk of overhanging dirt. *The dirt was loosening up.*

The thought of that made my hand close in on my shirt for something to grab hold of. As I did that I felt something in my shirt pocket. It was matches.

Then I did some thinking. I lit a match and held it under the piece of rabbit brush. It took hold and flamed. When I thought the flame was strong enough to stand a little breeze I heaved it up to the other brush ten feet above me.

The first try wasn't much good. The little piece of brush came back on me, burned me a little and then died. I tried it again and finally landed it up in the brush along the top of the bank. Then I held my breath.

A little flame shot up and then seemed to die down. "If that fire don't start," I said out loud, "I'm just as good as done for," which was the truth.

But it did start, slow but sure, and pretty soon I could see the sparks fly. Some of them fell on me and the horse but it was good to see that light and to hear the flames roar. I knew what rabbit brush would do once it got started burning. It would burn like a torch.

From then on instead of digging I waited. I felt sure somebody would ride up and look for me soon. Sure enough.

After a while, I heard somebody shout, my six-shooter barked out an answer and then I began to think . . . what if somebody should ride out upon the hunk of dirt that's hanging over me and start it down.

The thought of that got my lungs to working. "Stay back," I hollered, "stay back!"

"Where are you, Bill," somebody asked.

"In the bottom of the washout. But don't come near the edge of it where I am or it'll cave in. Get down from some other place."

I didn't have to tell them to hurry, they were doing that. Pretty soon half-a-dozen riders were digging me out with running irons used to brand with, six-shooters and everything they could get hold of. The horse was lifted off me and I was pulled up to where I could work my legs and get the blood circulating in them.

It took four saddle horses to pull my horse out. By the time I'd told the boys what happened I felt strong enough to stand up again. With the help of one of the boys I walked over to look at the hunk of earth that had been hanging over me all that long day. There was a crack in the ground which showed how ready it was to fall. I stuck my boot heel in the crack and shoved a little.

The earth seemed to go out from under us as that hunk left. A big cloud of dust went up, and when we looked again the washout was filled almost to the top.

Readings of Brands on Page 63

Ox Yoke

Reversed
K 5

Z
Quarter
Circle

S Wrench

H.T

T. S.

Shafter cross
T down

Six H
Double S

Quarter Circle O

(can be read either
way and is called
H.S)

Flying O
or Gushen

Centipede

ABOUT WILL JAMES

From Scribner's edition, published in 1938

Will James is a real cowboy and has lived most of his life on a ranch. When he was a very small boy he began to draw horses, and he has kept on drawing them eversince.

He is one of the most popular writers in the United States and has written many books for grown-ups and for boys and girls. His book Smoky, the Story of a Cowhorse won the Newbery medal.

Will James writes as a cowboy talks. In this book his writing has been somewhat changed in order to make the stories easier to read.

When he writes to his publishers, this cowboy author often draws funny pictures of himself at the end, or perhaps the head, of his letters.

Will James was born Joseph Ernest Nephtali Dufault in the province of Quebec on June 6, 1892. He left home as a teenager to live out his dream of becoming a cowboy in the American West. James went on to write and illustrate twenty-four books and numerous magazine articles about horses, cowboying, and the West. His works consistently captured the imagination of the public. He died in 1942, at the age of fifty.

We encourage you to patronize your local bookstore. Most stores will order any title that they do not stock. You may also order directly from Mountain Press using the order form provided below or by calling our toll-free number and using your credit card. We will gladly send you a free catalog upon request.

Other fine Cowboy and Western Americana Titles:

_____	Cowboys North and South	14.00/paper	25.00/cloth
_____	The Drifting Cowboy	14.00/paper	25.00/cloth
_____	Smoky, the Cowhorse	16.00/paper	36.00/cloth
_____	Cow Country	14.00/paper	25.00/cloth
_____	Sand	16.00/paper	30.00/cloth
_____	Lone Cowboy	16.00/paper	30.00/cloth
_____	Sun Up	16.00/paper	30.00/cloth
_____	Big-Enough	16.00/paper	30.00/cloth
_____	Uncle Bill	14.00/paper	26.00/cloth
_____	All in the Day's Riding	16.00/paper	30.00/cloth
_____	The Three Mustangeers	15.00/paper	30.00/cloth
_____	Home Ranch	16.00/paper	30.00/cloth
_____	Young Cowboy		15.00/cloth
_____	In the Saddle with Uncle Bill	14.00/paper	26.00/cloth
_____	Scorpion, A Good Bad Horse	15.00/paper	30.00/cloth
_____	Cowboy in the Making		15.00/cloth
_____	Flint Spears, Cowboy Rodeo Contestant	15.00/paper	30.00/cloth
_____	Look-See with Uncle Bill	14.00/paper	26.00/cloth
_____	The Will James Cowboy Book		18.00/cloth
_____	Ride for the High Points:		
	The Real Story of Will James (Jim Bramlett)	20.00/paper	
_____	The Will James Books: A Descriptive Bibliography		
	for Enthusiasts and Collectors (Don Frazier)	18.00/paper	

Please include $3.00 per order to cover postage and handling.

Please send the books marked above. I have enclosed $ _____

Name _____

Address _____

City/State/Zip_____

☐ Payment enclosed (check or money order in U.S. funds)

Bill my: ☐ VISA   ☐ MasterCard   ☐ American Express   ☐ Discover

Expiration Date: _____

Card No _____

Signature _____

MOUNTAIN PRESS PUBLISHING COMPANY
P. O. Box 2399 • Missoula, MT 59806
Order Toll-Free 1-800-234-5308 • _Have your credit card ready_
e-mail: info@mtnpress.com • website: www.mountain-press.com